y 398
2 .1
.09
.43
Grimm

Grimm, Jacob, 1785-1863.
[Wolf and the seven little kids]
The wolf and the seven little kids / the Brothers
Grimm ; illustrated by Martin Ursell ; text by Linda M.
Jennings. -- Morristown, N.J. : Silver Burdett Co.,
1986.
[28] p. : col. ill. ; 30 cm.

Translated from the German.
0289940X   LC:86006629   ISBN:0382093062

I. Grimm, Wilhelm, 1786-1859. II. Jennings, Linda,
(SEE NEXT CARD)

648   91FEB21   30/ci   1 00415733

FOR SHIRLEY AND STEVE

Library of Congress Cataloging-in-Publication Data
Wolf und die sieben jungen Geisslein. English.
   The wolf and the seven little kids.

   Translation of: Wolf und die sieben jungen Geisslein.
   Summary: Mother Goat rescues six of her kids
after they are swallowed by a wicked wolf.
   [1. Fairy tales. 2. Folklore – Germany] I. Grimm,
Jacob, 1785-1863. II. Grimm, Wilhelm, 1786-1859. III.
Ursell, Martin, ill. IV. Jennings, Linda, 1937-. V. Title.
VI. Title: Wolf and the 7 little kids.
PZ8.W815 1986   398.2′45297358 [E]   86-6629
ISBN 0-382-09306-2

Text copyright © 1986 Hodder and Stoughton Ltd
Illustrations copyright © 1986 Martin Ursell

Published in the United States in 1986
by Silver Burdett Company,
Morristown, New Jersey

Text by Linda M. Jennings

First published 1986 by Hodder and Stoughton Children's Books,
a division of Hodder and Stoughton Ltd,
Mill Road, Dunton Green, Sevenoaks, Kent TN 13 2YJ

Printed in Italy

THE BROTHERS GRIMM

THE WOLF AND THE SEVEN LITTLE KIDS

Illustrated by
MARTIN URSELL

Text by Linda M. Jennings

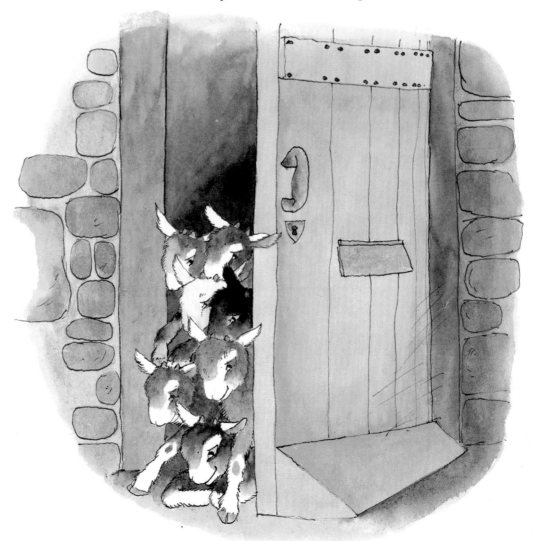

Silver Burdett Company · Morristown, New Jersey

There was once a nanny goat who had seven little kids. She loved her children dearly, and was concerned for their safety, but one day she was forced to go into the forest to search for food, leaving them at home alone. Before she went she called the little kids to her and said, "You must on no account open the door to anyone while I am away. Be especially careful of the old wolf, for he is a sly one and uses many disguises. If *he* should get into the cottage then that would be the end of you all. You will know him by his gruff voice and brown paws." The kids promised to do as their mother told them, and she went off, reassured.

The nanny goat had not long disappeared through the trees when the old wolf passed by. He had noticed the nanny goat leaving the cottage, so he quickly crept up to the door and knocked.

"Open the door, my dears," he said, "for here I am home again."

"Who are you?" asked the little kids.

"Why, your mother, of course," replied the wolf.

"You are not our mother, for her voice is soft and gentle, and yours is rough and gruff. You are the WOLF."

The wolf gave a howl of rage, and ran off into the forest.

But he was soon plotting and planning as to how he could trick his way back into the cottage. "What I need," he thought to himself, "is some chalk to make my voice sound soft." So off he went to a store where he purchased some pieces of chalk, which he swallowed. The shopkeeper watched him in amazement, not knowing what wicked plans the old wolf was hatching.

"Well, there is no accounting for taste," said the storekeeper, shaking his head.

Back to the cottage went the wolf, and, putting his paws on the windowsill, he tapped gently at the pane.

"Open the door, my darlings," cried the wolf in a soft, gentle voice. "It's your mother at last, with gifts for every one of you."

"You're not our mother," said the little kids, "for we can see your paws on the windowsill. Our mother's feet are snowy-white, but yours are brown. You are the WOLF."

Determined not to be defeated, the wolf raced off to the village as fast as his four legs would carry him. Into the bakery he ran and asked that his paws be covered with flour, so that they would appear snow-white. "Now I have them," thought the wolf, gleefully, and his mouth watered in anticipation of the feast he would enjoy.

"Open the door, my sweethearts," he called through the mail box of the cottage, "for your mother returns with food for a feast."

Now when the little kids heard the wolf's soft voice they said to him: "You have our mother's voice, but what of your paws?" The wolf placed his flour-covered paws on the windowsill.

"It's mother all right," cried the eldest kid, and he opened the door. When he saw who it was on the other side he gave a piteous bleat and tried to shut it in the wolf's face, but too late! With a bound the wolf was inside and, though the kids tried to hide – one under the table, one in the bed, the third in the stove, the fourth in the kitchen, the fifth under the sink, the sixth in the cupboard, and the seventh in the clock-case – SNAP! SNAP! SNAP! he found them all, save the seventh and the youngest.

With six little kids inside his stomach the old wolf was feeling very full and sleepy. Slowly he waddled out of the cottage and into a field where he found a quiet and shady spot under a tree. Soon he was snoring away, well satisfied with his morning's work.

Presently the nanny goat returned, and was horrified to find the door swinging open and the kitchen turned upside-down. There was no sign of her family. Then, suddenly, from out of the clock-case sprang the youngest kid, and he told his mother the whole terrible tale. "We may yet be in time," the little kid told his weeping mother, "if we can find the wolf."

The two of them hurried into the field, and very soon they heard a
loud sound coming from under a large tree. It was a roaring, snoring
kind of noise, and as they came closer they could see that it was the old
wolf, fast asleep. And, as they looked at him, they noticed that
something was moving inside his stomach.

"Quick, quick," said the nanny goat. "Go back to the cottage and
fetch me some scissors, needle and thread."

When the seventh little kid returned to the field with the scissors, needle and thread, his mother set to work. SNIP, SNIP, she went, and cut a large hole in the sleeping wolf's stomach. And oh, how wonderful! Out of the hole sprang all six little kids, none the worse for their terrible experience. How they danced for joy when they saw the sky and trees again and their dear mother standing near!

"There's no time to waste," said the nanny goat, "for any minute now the wolf may wake." Quickly she sent all the little kids to fetch some heavy stones, and as they brought them back to her she placed them in the hole in the wolf's stomach. Then she sewed up the hole neatly, and all the family scurried off behind the hedge to watch what would happen.

Very soon the wolf woke up, stretched himself, and staggered to his feet. "How thirsty I am," he thought. Slowly he lumbered off to a nearby well. As he stooped to drink he lost his balance and, because he was so full of heavy stones instead of nice, succulent little kids, he fell right in, and sank down, down, down to the bottom and was drowned. Immediately the nanny goat and her kids came running from behind the hedge.

"The wolf is dead, the wolf is dead," they all cried, and danced around the well, rejoicing at their good fortune.